Six-Minute
MYSTERIES

❖ ❖ ❖ ❖ ❖ ❖ ❖

by
Don Wulffson

illustrated by
Laurel Long

Lowell 🏠 House
Juvenile
Los Angeles

CONTEMPORARY BOOKS
Chicago

For my wife, Pam, with love
—*D.W.*

Publisher: Jack Artenstein
General Manager, Juvenile Division: Elizabeth Duell Wood
Editorial Director: Brenda Pope-Ostrow
Director of Publishing Services: Mary D. Aarons
Project Editor: Barbara Schoichet
Cover Designer: Lisa-Theresa Lenthall
Text Designer: Carolyn Wendt

Library of Congress Catalog Card Number: 94-26817

ISBN: 1-56565-169-3

10 9 8 7 6 5 4 3 2 1

CONTENTS

Wrong Move 5

The Mystery of Titan 11

The Death of the Party......................19

By the Book 27

Mysterious Smiles.............................35

The Mystery of the Mary Celeste..........43

The Broken Window............................51

An Unlucky Number 59

The Sunken Boat...............................67

The Radar-Brain Detective....................73

Framed 81

The Man in the Glass Bubble...............89

WRONG MOVE

❖ ❖ ❖ ❖ ❖ ❖ ❖

Kenya Williams and his granddad had character, intelligence, and a sense of fair play going for them—but not much in the way of material wealth or good fortune. Kenya, sixteen, and his granddad, Martin, seventy-four, lived in a second-story one-bedroom apartment in the meanest part of South-Central L.A. Martin Williams, partially crippled by a stroke, lived on his Social Security benefits and had trouble making ends meet for himself, let alone his grandson. Aware of the need to help out, Kenya chipped in working part-time after school and on weekends as a groundskeeper at Jordan High School, which he attended and where he maintained a B+ average. Someday Kenya hoped to become a cop, or maybe even make detective.

The sound of yelling, fighting, and even of gunfire was not uncommon in Kenya's neighborhood. Mostly, Kenya and his granddad ignored it. It was far away—usually—and there was nothing they could do about it.

But tonight was different.

Something was going on in the alley right below their apartment. There was the sound of an argument. Then of glass breaking. A fight followed. Then more yelling, a thudding noise, and a cry for help.

Martin called the police. Kenya, baseball bat in hand, was out the door and bounding down into the dimly lit alley before his granddad could stop him.

There he came upon a red Corvette, its lights on, the driver's door open, and the motor off. On the ground lay a large man in blue jeans, jogging shoes, and a letterman's jacket. He seemed to be in his early twenties. He was lying next to a telephone pole, unconscious. Near him, on the ground, lay a three-foot length of re-bar, reinforcement rod used in construction. Dazed, leaning against the car, the windshield of which was smashed, was a small, good-looking man. He was well dressed and probably in his mid-thirties. Pawing at a swollen jaw, the man looked groggily at Kenya as he approached.

"What's going on?" asked Kenya cautiously.

"I was comin' down to see a friend," said the small man, breathing heavily, trying to catch his breath. "I was going slow, looking for an address." He pointed to the big man on the ground. "Then that dude tried to steal my car. He smashed my windshield and told me to get out. He was about to smash in my head with that." He pointed to the re-bar. "We fought . . . and somehow I got it away from him." The small man shook his head. "Man, he's a big guy! Guess I got lucky."

"So you're okay?" Kenya asked, still keeping his distance.

"Yeah, except for a sore chin and busted windshield, I'm fine." He twirled keys on a key ring in the shape of a basketball hoop. "Thanks for—"

"Kenya, would you let the police handle this?"

Kenya turned around and saw his granddad making his way toward them on crutches. Other onlookers were peering out of back windows, and a few passersby had stopped and were taking in the scene.

"They should be here any minute," his granddad said, leaning on his crutches. "See?" he added at the sound of an approaching siren. "So let's all just sit tight." He glanced nervously at the two wounded men, then pulled his grandson next to him.

Shortly, the twin beams of headlights splashed across the walls of the alley. Then a squad car lit up the night with its red, blue, and white strobe as it roared up and came to a skidding stop in front of Kenya, his granddad, and the two men.

"What happened here?" demanded Sergeant Joseph Garcia.

The small man again explained what had happened.

Garcia's partner, Marlena Case, knelt down beside the large man to examine his wounds. "This one needs an ambulance, Joe," she said.

Garcia radioed for medical assistance while Case cuffed the still unconscious man on the ground.

"How about my windshield?" the small man asked the female officer as she got to her feet.

"Not much we—or you—can do about that," Case said, "but after we get this guy down to County Hospital, come down to the Third Precinct and file a complaint."

An ambulance arrived, and the two officers filled in the paramedics as they hefted the big man onto a gurney.

Kenya watched as the small man brushed broken glass off the front seat of the Corvette and climbed in behind the wheel. For a moment, the man looked confused, then pushed the control button to slide the seat forward and started the engine.

"Thanks," he called out to the officers, who were still talking to the paramedics. "I'll meet you at the police station."

"Wait!" yelled Kenya to the small man. Then he turned to the police officers. "Don't let him go!"

"Why?" asked the cops, almost in unison.

"This thing's all turned around," explained Kenya.

"What do you mean, Kenya?" asked his granddad.

The cops looked puzzled. The small man looked worried and very tense.

"This is the other guy's Corvette, not his!" Kenya aimed a finger at the small man. "A tall man would have the seat back; this guy's short—and had to slide the seat forward. He was the one trying to steal the car; otherwise, that seat would have already been forward."

"Kid's got a point," said Officer Case.

Garcia drew his gun. "Loop those fingers behind your head!" he ordered the small man. "Outta the car—slowly—and put your hands on the hood." Almost in one motion, Garcia cuffed the small man and pulled a wallet from his back pocket. He passed the wallet to Case.

"Jerome Lane is his name," said Case, looking in the wallet. She went around to the other side of the car. Flashlight in hand, she pulled out papers from the glove compartment. "Don't see the registration, but we've got insurance papers here for Maximillian Palmer." She nodded in the direction of the big man on the gurney, being attended to by the paramedics. "And that is Maximillian Palmer, according to the driver's license I pulled out of his wallet."

The small man, glaring angrily at Kenya, was read his rights and then loaded into the back of the patrol car.

"Good work, young man," said Garcia, clapping Kenya on the shoulder. "We almost blew it. Thanks."

"I kind of had my doubts from the beginning," said Kenya.

"How's that?" asked his granddad.

Kenya smiled at his granddad, then walked over to the Corvette and pulled the keys from the ignition. "The big guy had a letterman's jacket on—for basketball. And his key ring is in the shape of a basketball hoop. But it wasn't until the other guy got behind the wheel and had to bring the seat forward—way forward—that I was sure."

Martin Williams put his arm around his grandson and beamed. "He's a fine young man," he boasted to the cops.

"Got my vote," said Officer Case.

"You've got a good head on your shoulders, son," said Garcia. "Ever consider going into police work?"

Kenya laughed. "Yeah, maybe I'll try to make detective."

THE MYSTERY OF TITAN

❖ ❖ ❖ ❖ ❖ ❖ ❖

Tanya Ling was extremely proud of her dad. He had verified that Titan, the largest and brightest of Saturn's ten satellites, possessed an atmosphere. Then, using unmanned space probes, he determined that Titan's atmosphere could sustain human life and that the satellite was rich in zinium, a metal far stronger and, in many ways, more precious than diamonds. Finally, it had been her father's concept, his vision, to send settlers to Titan, to colonize the satellite and begin mining operations there.

All had been going well. Thirty-one colonists had set up a di-trobe dome in which to live. Mining had begun. Unmanned space freighters had been readied to carry the precious cargo to Earth. The colonists had reported no problems. Then suddenly a disturbing transmission came. It was garbled, distorted, and frightening. Tanya remembered listening to her dad, in his study, playing a recording of the transmission over and over: "Beasts . . . everywhere . . . jelly . . . slime . . . kill us!" There had been no further transmissions from Titan ever since.

11

"It's obvious, honey," Edward Ling had confided in his daughter, "that there are living creatures on Titan. Apparently they have killed the colonists. But we're not beat yet!"

It took only two months to get a second manned flight to Titan funded and under way. This time fifty-four soldiers armed with the latest weaponry were sent to the satellite. Their goal: to find any survivors, and to wipe out the beasts on Titan.

The flight went well. Upon landing, the soldiers found the colony all but destroyed. The dome, where the colonists had lived, and the mines, where they had worked, were in a shambles. Not a single surviving colonist was found, nor were their remains. But the soldiers did find the beasts of Titan—red, slimy, jelly-like creatures, which undoubtedly had killed and eaten the humans.

Day after day the soldiers engaged the horrible creatures in battle. The body count was transmitted back to Earth from the colonel in charge. On day one he reported six beasts killed; day two, seven killed; day three, eleven killed and four wounded; day four, two killed and one wounded. On the fifth day, and thereafter, the colonel reported that there were no further contacts with the enemy. Possibly all had been killed; or, more probably, the rest had withdrawn and were in hiding. The only other occurrence of note was that the wounded beasts, all five of them, had died in captivity. Like the other dead, they were all cremated.

More than half the soldiers were set to work mining, while the others stood guard or scouted the satellite for more of the beasts. Zinium ore was hacked

and drilled, graded, and readied for transport to Earth. Transmissions to Earth were clear and on schedule, and there were no reports of any unusual problems . . . except that some of the soldiers complained of headaches, rashes, and homesickness. All seemed to be going well.

And then the transmissions stopped again.

For two days, ground control frantically tried to make contact. Not until late on the third day were the soldiers heard from. The transmission was as shocking, disturbing, and incomprehensible as the one sent by the first group of colonists: "Everywhere slime . . . eat flesh . . . brains . . . no stopping . . . too fast . . . !" After that, nothing but silence.

A third contingent of soldiers, one hundred strong, was sent to Titan to find out what happened and rescue any survivors. They killed thirty-nine aliens, wounded nine, and captured six. As before, all the wounded and captured also subsequently died, and were cremated. As for the soldiers of the third contingent, there was not a single casualty.

But the sigh of relief on Earth did not last long. Shortly thereafter, a garbled transmission—similar to the ones sent by the first two contingents—came, followed by complete silence.

Each day Tanya watched the strain increasing on her father's face when he came home from work. Neither he nor anyone else had been able to figure out what was wiping out the colonists, the force of fifty-four well-armed soldiers that followed, or the most recent expeditionary force of soldiers. What had they been up against? What had attacked them? What sort of horrid battles had they fought . . . and finally lost?

In short, what was the solution to the riddle of Titan?

An answer had to be found.

"The only way we can find out what happens up there," Edward Ling told his daughter one day after work, "is to send another—even larger—force to Titan. In fact, today we received presidential approval for a force of five thousand more troops."

That night, Edward Ling went to bed early. Unable to sleep, Tanya went to her dad's study. She listened to recordings, studied computer printouts, and pored over facts, figures, names, and dates. She was bleary-eyed, exhausted, and it was almost morning when she saw it. She stared in shock; it—the answer—was right there in front of her. And it was all so simple.

"I've got it!" she exclaimed, rushing into her father's bedroom and shaking him awake.

"Got what?" he asked drowsily, yawning.

"The answer to what happens on Titan—the solution to the mystery!"

Mr. Ling sat up and stared at his daughter.

"It's mostly a question of numbers," said Tanya, a calculator in one hand and a sheaf of papers in the other.

Her father gave her a puzzled look, then nodded, gesturing for her to continue.

"How many settlers were in the first colony?" she asked.

15

"Thirty-one."

"And how many in the second flight—the military expedition?"

"Fifty-four."

"Do you know what I'm getting at?" asked Tanya.

"I haven't got a clue," her father said.

Tanya sat down on the bed. "We lost a total of eighty-five people in the first two expeditions. Compare that with the body count—the total of jellylike aliens killed by our forces. Eighty-five! The exact same number! Do you see now what I'm telling you, Dad?"

"I'm starting to. And it's scaring the devil out of me!"

Tanya continued. "The people complained of headaches and rashes—then something suddenly happened up there. There were the same strange transmissions, as though the senders had all but lost their minds, and then no transmissions at all. Something happens—something sudden—in that place, on that satellite. I don't know exactly what. But they change—humans change into jellylike blobs."

"Which means," said Edward Ling, "that each time we've gone up there to kill aliens, what we've really been killing is our own people—who have mutated into monsters!" He frowned. "Why, their brains must have been deteriorating as rapidly as their bodies—before they could communicate in an understandable way what had happened to them!"

"I think you're right, Dad," said Tanya. "But what do you think caused the mutation?"

"Exposure to zinium, possibly. However, we'll probably never know for sure." He sighed.

16

"Regardless of the cause, one thing we do know is that the same thing has happened—or is happening—to the last group of a hundred soldiers sent to Titan. And there's nothing we can do to save them."

"But there is something we can do to save the five thousand soldiers being readied to go to Titan," said Tanya.

Edward Ling was on the phone almost instantly. Tanya sat quietly and listened as her father explained the solution to the puzzle of Titan to the president.

"So you see, sir," her father concluded, "no further missions should be sent to Titan, nor should any zinium ever be brought to Earth." Then he told the president who had solved the riddle. Smiling, Edward Ling held out the phone to his daughter. "Tanya," he said, "someone would like to speak to you."

THE DEATH OF THE PARTY

❖ ❖ ❖ ❖ ❖ ❖ ❖

Sixteen-year-old Barbara Paisley was having the time of her life. She had the greatest summer job a teenager could hope for. She was an assistant make-up artist for Crystal Rock Pictures. The company was filming a sci-fi thriller called Isle of Pain on an isolated stretch of beach in about the greatest place in the world, beautiful Barbuda Island in the Caribbean.

The only bad part of the job was working with Alice Wilder, one of the actresses in the movie. She could be sweet and pleasant one moment, then a spoiled brat the next, endlessly complaining about everybody and everything. Sometimes when Barbara applied Alice's makeup, trimmed her red-brown curly hair, or manicured her nails, Alice would heap praise on Barbara. Then, the next time around, doing exactly the same work in exactly the same way, Alice would fly into a rage, yelling and cursing that Barbara had made her look "hideous."

Barbara never said anything. She would just smile pleasantly and tackle the job again until Alice the Terrible was satisfied.

By the sixth week of shooting, Alice's part in the movie was complete except for a final scene and a couple of retakes. The character she played died early in the movie, so after "dying" a few more times until the director yelled, "Cut and print," Alice would head for home. Then, thankfully, Barbara would be assigned to another actor.

During her first weeks, Barbara's schedule was always the same. She had to be up by 6:00 A.M. to get things in order in the makeup trailer. Alice would wander in anywhere between seven and ten, Barbara would get her ready for the day's shoot, and then, along with other behind-the-scenes people, Barbara would go to the shoot location, ready to take care of any touch-ups needed between takes. From twelve-thirty to two-thirty everyone broke for lunch—to eat, relax, and get ready for the next scene to be filmed.

In the beginning, Barbara really enjoyed these midday breaks, and would have a long, leisurely swim in the warm, emerald green waters of the lagoon fronting the isolated patch of the island. Then she'd have a quick bite to eat and be back to work, usually before the others.

But lately, as Alice Wilder's part in the movie was coming to an end, the fussy actress had been demanding special attention. She wanted to be taken care of in the privacy of her own trailer instead of in the makeup room. Instead of coming back from her break at two-thirty, Barbara was now ordered to report back to work at exactly two. That soon turned into one-thirty, then one, and today, on the last day Alice was supposed to be on the island, she told

Barbara to be there by twelve forty-five—not to do her makeup, but to pack for her! This left Barbara only fifteen minutes to wolf down her lunch, then hurry over to do Alice's dirty work for her.

"Well, at least this is her last day," Barbara grumbled to herself as she knocked softly on Alice's aluminum trailer door.

When there was no answer, she called out, then walked in.

For a moment, all Barbara could do was stare. Alice Wilder lay in a corner—a pair of scissors shoved deep into her heart. Her lifeless eyes, glassy and blank, were staring at the ceiling.

Stifling the urge to be sick, Barbara got down on her knees and felt for a pulse. Finding none, she snatched up a cellular phone and called Rodney Devlin, head of security. He was there in a flash.

"Man," said Rodney, shaking his head at the sight, "somebody sure hated her."

"Just about everybody," said Barbara.

"Oh?" asked Rodney, raising his eyebrows. "Such as?"

"Such as James Cole, the screenwriter she was always putting down in front of everybody. And Mandy Dennis, who originally had Alice's part in the movie, until Alice 'pulled a few strings.' Then there's Damon Rider. He was in love with Alice, but she dumped him for Elton Collins." Barbara shrugged. "The list goes on and on. To be honest, just about everybody on this island had a motive for killing Alice the Terrible."

"Do you suspect anyone in particular?" asked Rodney.

"Only the one person she had a real hold on."

Rodney wrinkled his brow. "And just what is that supposed to mean?"

"Not much, unless we play this thing right."

Rodney really looked puzzled now. "You're talking in circles around me," he said, picking up his cellular phone. "I can't go on your silly guesses or on hunches—especially when you're not attaching names." He punched a number into the phone. "I'm calling the police."

"Don't call anybody," said Barbara, grabbing the phone from Rodney's hand.

"And why not?" asked Rodney. "It is my job, you know."

"Because there're only a handful of people on this island. And one of them is the murderer."

"Obviously," said Rodney, a bit irritated, "and the police will find out who."

"But I've got a plan," said Barbara. "I think I can help you find the murderer without the police."

"And how are you going to do that?" Rodney asked, clearly interested in being a hero.

"First off, we don't let anybody know Alice is dead."

Rodney scratched his head. "But why?"

"You'll see," said Barbara, grinning. "You'll see after the party."

That night there was a dinner and dance for everybody involved in the production of Isle of Pain. Grips and stunt people mixed with actors, writers, and directors. Attire was informal, so everybody showed up in sandals, lightweight gowns, tropical suits, and jurachis, colorful cotton shorts and shirts. Large umbrella-covered tables decorated with flowers formed two semicircles near a barbecue pit, and in front of a makeshift bandstand, a small hardwood floor had been set in place for dancing.

Obviously, Alice Wilder did not turn up for the party, and Rodney Devlin, as Barbara had told him to do, went from person to person, asking if they knew anything of her whereabouts. Most seemed to be having too good a time to even give Rodney much of an answer. Others were simply indifferent to the unfriendly actress's whereabouts. But the question did make one man quite nervous. That man was Harold Lindon, the film's producer.

Barbara watched Lindon with interest—especially when Alice Wilder actually did arrive at the party. That's when Lindon nearly went into shock. A bit overdressed, as pretty and flamboyant-looking as ever, Alice made her way slowly across the dance floor toward the producer, now white as chalk. He backed away as she continued to approach, then stumbled, fell over a chair, and scrambled to his feet.

The music stopped, and all eyes turned on Lindon . . . and the steadily approaching Alice Wilder.

"But—but you're dead!" he screamed, turning and running right into the arms of Rodney Devlin.

"Alice" removed a red-brown wig, pulled off a putty nose, and stripped off a latex mask. Now Barbara Paisley looked evenly at Lindon. "I don't know exactly how the murder happened, but I know you killed Alice Wilder, Mr. Lindon. No one else knew she was dead—or was surprised to see her here tonight. Only you, Mr. Lindon, looked like you'd seen a ghost." She paused for a few minutes and stared at the shaking producer. "Alice threatened to back out of doing her last scene, didn't she?" Barbara asked.

Lindon, still speechless, nodded.

"She probably demanded—extorted—more money out of you for doing the scene, am I right?" Barbara pressed.

"Fifty thousand," said Lindon. "I—I didn't have the extra money, and—"

"And if she had not done the scene, your movie—your entire investment—would have been wiped out."

Just then, two Barbudan police officers, who had mixed with the crowd, stepped forward and handcuffed the unresisting producer.

Barbara had to laugh. If Alice, true to form, hadn't been the "death of the party," Lindon might have gotten away with murder.

BY THE BOOK

❖ ❖ ❖ ❖ ❖ ❖ ❖

Melissa Winthrop had worked for the Knights on the Triple-J Ranch as long as Jimmy could remember. She did the cooking, cleaning, washing, and ironing. The woman was a writer, too—or at least she wanted to be one. Over the years, she had written half a dozen murder mysteries—none of which had been published. When Jimmy was just a little boy, Melissa, then a young woman, would always talk about how she was going to "make it big one day." But now Jimmy was sixteen and Melissa, in her forties, still had no publisher who had shown even the slightest interest in her work.

The woman's failure to publish, it seemed to Jimmy, had done something to her mind. The more her books were rejected, the more frantically she tackled her writing. Her small, private bedroom on the ranch was just below Jimmy's, and he would hear her pecking away at the typewriter at all hours of the night. The next day, the poor obsessed woman—often with circles under her eyes—would do her regular chores, always pestering whomever she could corner

27

while she talked about her latest murder mystery.

But the Triple-J was a working ranch. Jimmy, his two sisters, Janice and Janine, and his mom and dad put in long hours, and they had only a limited amount of time—and a limited amount of patience—for Melissa's endless prattling about her quest to be an author. Jimmy's dad made it clear to her that she was free to write all she wanted, and he wished her the best of luck, but she was not to let her writing in any way interfere with her work—or anybody else's work—at the ranch.

In a way, Jimmy felt sorry for Melissa. She had failed in her life's dream—and it was obviously making her crazy. She did her chores at a nervous pace; sometimes talking to herself, and now and then actually scolding herself for making a mistake of some kind. And more and more frequently, she began lashing out at Jimmy and the rest of his family over odd things, such as walking in the room when she didn't expect them, or walking up behind her too quietly.

Finally, Jimmy's parents threatened to fire her over her outbursts. She apologized, promised to control her temper, and begged them for another chance. Despite their doubts, they let her stay on.

Almost overnight, Melissa's outbursts stopped. In fact, little by little, a change came over the woman. Though still a bit strange in her ways, now, more often than not, she had a smile on her face, and her spirits seemed to have definitely picked up.

"I'm writing a new book," she told everyone, "and it's unlike anything I've ever done before. It's unlike anything anyone has ever done before."

The entire Knight family was happy to see Melissa in good spirits and tried to support her. But whenever anyone questioned her about the new book, an odd look appeared in her eye, and a funny little smile twisted onto her face.

Jimmy had read some of Melissa's other manuscripts, but this book she would not show to anyone. This book, unlike the others, she would hardly even speak about. She'd even change the subject if anyone asked her too many questions about it. It was as though the book, to Melissa, was some sort of weird, private secret.

"Come on, Melissa, what's it about?" asked Jimmy one wintry afternoon as the odd housekeeper worked in the kitchen baking Christmas cookies and cakes for the annual Triple-J Christmas party.

"It's very scary," she said, and that was all . . . except she added, "I named it after the Christmas carol 'Silent Night.'"

"That's the title?" asked Jimmy.

"Sort of," Melissa answered as she greased a pan.

Puzzled by Melissa's odd answer, Jimmy persisted in asking her what the book was about.

For a long while it seemed she wasn't going to answer. Then, finally, she said, "A murder—actually, several murders."

"Where does the novel take place?" Jimmy asked eagerly, glad he'd finally gotten her going.

Melissa kneaded some dough, gazed into space, and smiled. "It's not a novel. It's nonfiction, you might say." She stopped work for a moment and looked into Jimmy's eyes intently. "Did you know, Jimmy, that life imitates art, and that art, at the same time, imitates life? The two are all mixed up together."

A bit taken aback by the strange answer, Jimmy fell silent. He was about to get up and leave when Melissa suddenly broke into a wide grin. "For almost twenty years I've been writing," she said with a weird chuckle. "But now I've finally found the perfect story—a book that every publisher will want. No doubt about it, my boy. This one will be a guaranteed best-seller!"

"How come?" asked Jimmy. "How do you know?"

Melissa shrugged, went back to work, and began humming "Silent Night."

The following day, Christmas Eve, Melissa went into town with Jimmy's mother and sisters to do grocery shopping. Jimmy had no trouble picking the simple lock to Melissa's bedroom, and no trouble finding the mysterious manuscript—under the bed, where she kept all her other attempts at writing. But he was startled when he looked at the large stack of papers. Melissa had written the book in code!

The first sentence began: SILENT OT TISH YORST. And there was another oddity. The book had a dedication on the second page, written in readable words. It said: "To Ana Gram, whose book will be the first and last word."

Jimmy glanced at his watch. He had only two hours before Melissa got back. Maybe he could break the code in that time and read—at least skim—through some of it.

Somehow, he was sure, the dedication was the key to the code. Ana Gram, though a name, is also a term for any word that could have its letters rearranged to make a new word. The first and last word of Melissa's book was listen, an anagram for "silent." Using this as a base, he unraveled the code.

The hair stood up on the back of his neck as he read the decoded title: Silent Knights. He was horrified when he finally figured out the first line: Listen to this story, this murder, written before it happened.

After about fifty pages, Jimmy had read all he needed to. He was just about to shove the manuscript back under the bed when he noticed something sticking out from under Melissa's mattress. It was a pistol! Now he was sure of Melissa's evil intentions. Leaving the pistol where it was, Jimmy ran off to where his dad was working in the barn. He explained what he had read, and what Silent Knights was about. Amazed that the old housekeeper could come up with such a horrific plot, Jimmy's father immediately called the state police.

When Jimmy's mom and sisters returned from shopping with Melissa, they were shocked to find state troopers waiting in the living room. Melissa stared fiery-eyed at Jimmy when she saw the manuscript of her book on the coffee table. She looked as if she were going to murder him with her eyes as one of the troopers handcuffed her.

"What's going on?" exclaimed Jimmy's mother.

Jimmy pointed to the manuscript. "The book that Melissa has been writing," he explained, "is about a horrible mass murder. It happens on Christmas Eve, which would be tonight. It happens on a ranch called the Triple-J. And the people killed are Janice, Janine, and Jimmy Knight—and their parents."

Janice turned to Melissa. "You were planning to murder us?" she asked, her voice shaking.

"So many of the books they sell these days are about true crimes," said Melissa, a faraway look in her eyes. "But mine would have been the best! Instead of being written after the murder, this one was written before. Famous!" she cried. "I would have been famous!"

Jimmy and his family watched as the troopers escorted Melissa from the house and out to the patrol car.

"It's so frightening—and sad," said Jimmy. "She planned a murder just to get a book published."

His dad put his arm around him. "And you, son, saved our lives by solving a murder that never happened."

MYSTERIOUS SMILES

❖ ❖ ❖ ❖ ❖ ❖ ❖

For as long as Bruno Peruggia could remember, he'd lived at St. Alban's Home for Children in Paris, France. All his life he had been haunted by the fact that he knew almost nothing of his past. He knew only that his name was Peruggia, that his parents had died in an auto accident when he was two years old, and that he had an aunt named Angela Giocondo. This aunt paid for his room and board at St. Alban's and even sent him gifts on his birthday and at Christmas, but she had never come to see him.

One day in his history class, Bruno's teacher was talking about probably the most famous portrait in the world—that of the Mona Lisa. The teacher said that the painting, completed in 1504, was done by Leonardo Da Vinci, and it now hung in the Louvre Museum in Paris. The portrait, Bruno's teacher explained, was of a real person, the wife of a wealthy Italian merchant, Lisa del Giocondo.

The name shocked Bruno: Giocondo was his aunt's last name. Was it possible that his aunt, Angela Giocondo, was related to Lisa Giocondo—the original

Mona Lisa? If it were true, then he, Bruno Peruggia, had quite a heritage!

Excited to learn about his past, Bruno went to the St. Alban's library, where he read everything he could get his hands on about the Mona Lisa. He learned that the Giocondos, an Italian family, paid Da Vinci a large sum for the portrait, but that somehow the painting mysteriously ended up in France several years later. Rumor had it that the French royal family used their great wealth and influence to "rob" it from the Italians, to whom, by all rights, it really belonged.

Wanting to learn more, Bruno found a book about Da Vinci that gave a more detailed history of the famous portrait. Reading it, he was surprised to learn that the masterpiece had been stolen from the Louvre in the year 1911. The thief, an artist employed at the Louvre, stole it by walking out with it hidden under his coat. After keeping it for two years, giving no explanation for his actions, he turned himself in—and returned the painting to the Louvre.

To Bruno, the most shocking part of the whole story was the name of the thief—Vincenzo Peruggia. Peruggia was Bruno's last name! Now it was possible that he could be related to both the woman who posed for the Mona Lisa and the thief who stole it.

That afternoon, Bruno decided to find out. He went to see Sister Madeline, the director of St. Alban's, in her office.

"Please," he begged her, "please tell me who my parents were. Tell me about Angela Giocondo and Vincenzo Peruggia. I know Angela is my aunt, but why have I never met her?"

Sister Madeline shook her head and whispered, "I'm sorry, Bruno, but I am sworn to secrecy."

"Can you at least tell me where my aunt lives?" Bruno asked. "I know it's in France, but what part?"

"I'm sorry," said Sister Madeline. "I am not allowed to give you that information either."

"It's not fair!" protested Bruno. "I have a right to know about my past. I have a right to know who I am!" Angry, he stormed from the room.

For the rest of the day, Bruno thought about the whole thing, and by early evening he had made a decision—he was going to solve the mystery of his past, even if it meant running away from St. Alban's.

That night Bruno put his plan into motion. He crawled along a ledge of the main building of St. Alban's, and using a butter knife, he pried open a window into Sister Madeline's office. There, in a Rolodex file, he found that his aunt lived on an estate in Vanves, a town not far from Paris. Now he was well on his way to solving the mystery of his past.

Bruno was up bright and early the next morning. But before heading for Vanves, there was something else he had to do—something he had to see.

He took a bus to the Louvre. Dazzled by all the incredible works in the famous museum, Bruno was particularly interested in one piece of art.

Following the directions of a guard, he found his way into a huge, beautiful gallery filled with tourists. Most of their attention was on a single painting, the

Mona Lisa. Guarded by two men with automatic rifles, the beautiful portrait hung alone on a single wall. People from all over the world gazed at the painting in awe, and Bruno found himself doing the same. The face was lovely. But it was the smile that Bruno found most incredible. It was such a secretive, strange smile.

Who are you? wondered Bruno, staring at the odd woman in the portrait. And who am I? It seemed as though Mona Lisa were gazing back at him, as though she were smiling directly into his eyes, smiling because she held the secret to his life.

The train ride to Vanves took almost two hours, and it took another hour of walking and hitchhiking for Bruno to get to Angela Giocondo's home in the countryside. The old estate was huge, beautiful, and surrounded by a high wall. Bruno climbed a tree and crawled out onto a long branch. Just before dropping down on the other side of the wall, he saw a young woman sitting in the estate's garden. Though her face was partially veiled by fine black lace, she seemed oddly familiar.

Bruno's approach startled her. "Who are you?" she demanded, rising from where she was sitting.

"I am Bruno Peruggia," he said. "Are you my aunt? Are you Angela Giocondo?"

For a long moment the woman stared. "I do not know how you found me," she said softly, "but I know why you are here."

"I only want to know why you have taken care of me all these years," Bruno said, his eyes searching through the veil. "All my life, my past has been a mystery to me, and I think you can help me solve it. Please, Mademoiselle Giocondo, tell me who I am."

From behind the veil, tears coursed down the woman's cheeks. "I was hoping that you would never find me," she said, her soft voice choked with emotion. "But now that you are here, I can see the pain I have caused you by not telling you about your past." Angela Giocondo's hand went to a key that hung from a necklace made of gold and black velvet. "I will tell you everything—but only on the condition that you never reveal the secret to anyone."

"What secret?" asked Bruno, his eyes wide with wonder.

"Follow me," said Angela Giocondo, leading the way to the house. "I will show you."

In a richly decorated sitting room, servants brought tea and cakes. Nervous, Bruno sat down on a green-and-gold sofa opposite the mysterious woman.

"We are not to be disturbed," she told the servants, "under any circumstances."

Eager to get started, Bruno launched right in as soon as the servants left, explaining to his aunt all he knew so far. "I read that the last name of the real Mona Lisa is Giocondo—your last name," Bruno began, "and my name is Peruggia, the name of the man who stole the—"

"He did not steal it. Vincenzo Peruggia, your grandfather, merely took the painting—and he did so to honor someone's dying wish."

"Who?" asked Bruno.

"Lisa Giocondo," his aunt said. "The real Mona Lisa."

"But why would my grandfather, a Peruggia, do this for the Giocondos?" Bruno wanted to know.

The woman sighed. "The two families were—and still remain—very close," she explained. "The painting rightfully belonged to Lisa Giocondo—to her family, to my family. And, after centuries, your grandfather was finally able to fulfill her dying wish to have the painting back."

"I think I understand," said Bruno. "But what I can't figure out is why my grandfather returned the painting after keeping it for a full two years."

The trace of a smile was detectable behind Angela Giocondo's veil as she slipped the key from her necklace and made her way to a heavy wood door. "Why, indeed, would he take it from the museum and then return it? Many have asked the question, and you are about to know the answer," she said, unlocking the door and leading Bruno into a room, a beautiful room, perfectly kept like a shrine.

Speechless, Bruno stared at the only thing of importance in the room—a portrait of a woman . . . with a strange, mysterious smile. It looked exactly like the Mona Lisa painting he'd seen in the Louvre.

"I don't understand," Bruno said with a gasp.

"Think," said Mademoiselle Giocondo. "Think clearly about every detail you have been told . . . and about what you see before you."

"The Giocondos wanted the Mona Lisa back," he said. "My grandfather took it, then two years later

41

returned it."

"And what was your grandfather's occupation?"

Bruno's mouth dropped open. "A painter!" he exclaimed. "So when he gave the Mona Lisa back, what he was really giving them was—" He took a deep breath, unable to finish the statement.

At that moment, Angela Giocondo lifted her veil, revealing a beautiful face, not greatly different from that of Mona Lisa. Bruno could clearly see that his aunt's ancestry was evident in her facial features—especially in her smile.

Bruno kept looking from his aunt to the portrait. "My grandfather, a painter, had the Mona Lisa for two years—long enough to paint a copy. Are you saying that the painting I am looking at in this room is the real Mona Lisa . . . and the one thousands are going to see in the Louvre every day is a fake? Is that what you're saying?"

Angela Giocondo said nothing. But her mouth slowly formed into an odd, all-knowing, secretive smile, a smile that said it all.

THE MYSTERY
OF THE
MARY CELESTE

❖ ❖ ❖ ❖ ❖ ❖ ❖

Ricky Steel was surprised to find his mother in their apartment when he came home from school. Linda Steel, an assistant editor at Hadrian House Publishers, always worked long, hard hours and usually didn't get in until seven or later.

"Hi, Mom," said Ricky. "You're home early. What's up?"

Linda Steel, sitting at the kitchen table, looked up into the questioning eyes of her son. "Hi, kiddo," she said, then turned back to the old, weather-beaten book in front of her.

"What are you working on?" asked Ricky, getting a soda from the fridge.

"Something that's driving me nuts," his mother said. "Actually, it's a diary that's supposed to have been found in an attic here in New York City. If it's authentic, it solves one of the weirdest true mysteries of all time."

43

That got Ricky's attention. "What mystery is that?" he asked, taking a long swallow of soda.

"In December, 1872, the captain of a British ship, while crossing the Atlantic, spotted another ship, which was sailing in a strange, erratic manner," his mother explained. "When the captain hailed the ship, there was no response, and so he sent some of his crew over to investigate. As it turns out, the name of the sailing ship was the Mary Celeste, and though it was sailing along across the Atlantic out of New York, there wasn't a single person on board."

"Weird," said Ricky, pulling up a chair. "And you say this is supposed to be a true story?"

His mother nodded. "Later, it was found that there had originally been ten people aboard—the captain, Benjamin Briggs; his wife; their baby daughter; and a crew of seven. But the odd thing was, there had been no storms reported in that area of the Atlantic, and most everything seemed to be in good order on the ship. Chests of clothes were dry. There was plenty of food and water. The ship wasn't even leaking. And that's not even the most puzzling part of the mystery."

"What was?" asked Ricky, his eyes growing wide.

"Well," his mother said, obviously pleased that her son was taking such an interest, "though the ship wasn't sinking, all the lifeboats were gone. So the question is, why did all these people abandon a ship that wasn't even in trouble?"

"There must've been something wrong," said Ricky.

"That's true," his mother said. "The boarding party did find some minor damage. A compass was broken, some of the rigging was torn, and there were gashes in the railing. Over the years, there have been all sorts of theories as to what happened. One is that everyone on board went insane and jumped ship. Another is that a giant squid attacked the ship. Still others claim that pirates, or even aliens, scared everyone." She paused and smiled. "There have been all sorts of theories, but none of them—to this date—have panned out."

Ricky picked up the beaten-up old diary.

"Be careful with that, honey," Ricky's mother said, nervously taking the diary away from him. "It may be worth a lot to my publishing company." She carefully placed the old book back on the kitchen table. "Just a week ago, a woman came into my office claiming that the only survivor from the Mary Celeste

wrote it. She says she found the diary in her attic, glanced through it, and realized she had stumbled upon the whole story of what actually happened."

"And what's that?" asked Ricky. History was one of his favorite subjects.

"Supposedly, the diary was written by Ernst Stemmer, one of the crewmen aboard the ship. Stemmer wrote that Captain Briggs caught him stealing, the two got into a fight, and Stemmer killed Briggs with a hatchet. He then grabbed a pistol, killed two other crewmen, and ordered Mrs. Briggs and her baby and four other crewmen into a lifeboat. He set them adrift without food or water, and they all evidently perished at sea.

"For two days, Stemmer sailed alone," Ricky's mother continued. "Afraid of getting caught for murder, he stocked the one remaining lifeboat with provisions and rowed for land, which he reached in three days. Eventually, he made his way back to New York."

Ricky sat back looking satisfied as though he'd just read a good book. "Sounds like it could have happened that way. Don't you think?"

His mother nodded. "Yes, but is the diary itself authentic?" She frowned. "I've been given the job of determining if it's fake or real. The woman who brought it to us at Hadrian House wants twenty thousand. If we publish it and it is authentic, then we have a best-seller—and I come out looking great. But if we publish it and it's a fake, then we've not only wasted our money, but Hadrian House becomes the laughingstock of the publishing industry—and I'm probably out of a job."

"Have you had someone test the paper and ink to see how old they are?" asked Ricky.

"The experts confirm that the paper and ink are both very old. They also say the materials were of the kind that could have been bought around the year 1872, when the Mary Celeste was found."

"Then it's authentic?" asked Ricky.

"Not necessarily. By using old ink in an old blank diary, and by then applying moisture and a heat lamp to fade the ink, the whole thing could have been fabricated last week." She sighed. "So I have to decide its authenticity in some other way—by examining every word. So far, I can't find a thing wrong."

"Mind if I take a look at it?" asked Ricky. "I promise to be careful."

"Well, I have been staring at it until I'm cross-eyed. Maybe a break would do me good." She looked at her son sternly. "Remember: This diary—if it's real—is worth a lot to my company."

Ricky took over his mother's seat at the kitchen table and began studying the ancient, yellowing pages of the diary. Now and then he would look up a word in the dictionary or a fact or date in one of the reference books his mother had piled up on the table. In his school notebook, he made notes and copied down lines from the diary.

His mother had fallen asleep on the living room couch long before.

It was ten o'clock when Ricky gently nudged her

awake.

"I've got the answer, Mom," he said quietly, sitting down on the couch.

She blinked and looked at him sleepily. "Are you sure?" she asked.

Ricky handed her a page from his notebook. On it were written three lines he had copied from the book.

The body of Captain Briggs was lying in the back part of the ship.

I wiped up the blood with paper towels and tossed the hatchet overboard.

The sea was choppy as I started rowing the lifeboat toward the Hawaiian Islands, the nearest body of land, only some five nautical miles away.

"Read the lines a few times," Rick instructed his mother. "Each one proves this diary is a complete fake." He handed her the notebook.

"Do you see what's wrong in these lines?" he asked, when she had read them several times over.

"Maybe I'm too sleepy," his mother said, yawning as she handed him back the notebook. "Why don't you just tell me what you're getting at, kiddo?"

"In the first line," Ricky said, eager to explain his theory, "whoever wrote this mentioned, 'the back part of the ship.' A sailor would say 'the stern.'"

His mother smiled. "But maybe he was just an ignorant sailor."

Ricky frowned. "That's possible, I guess. But now look again at the second line. In this one the writer mentions paper towels." Ricky paused, waiting for his mother to catch on. "Don't you see? Paper towels weren't invented until 1907."

Linda Steel sat bolt upright. "And the Mary Celeste incident took place in 1872!"

"Which means," said Ricky, beaming proudly, "that whoever wrote this fake diary created a make-believe murderer who used paper towels thirty-five years before they were invented!"

"And the last one's the clincher," said Linda Steel, wide awake now.

"It sure is," said Ricky. "It mentions heading for the Hawaiian Islands."

His mother broke into a wide grin. "Which isn't possible. The Mary Celeste was in the Atlantic Ocean—and the Hawaiian Islands are in the Pacific!"

"So," Ricky concluded, "this whole diary is bogus."

"Ricky, you've saved your mother's life!" Linda Steel said excitedly. "Tomorrow is the big meeting where I give my report on whether Hadrian House should buy the rights to the diary or not. Everybody's going to be there—from the publisher to the woman who gave us the fake diary. I can't wait to see the expression on her face when I put the facts on the table." She put her arm around Ricky and gave him a big kiss on the cheek. "And I can't wait to tell everybody what a smart son I've got!"

THE BROKEN WINDOW

❖ ❖ ❖ ❖ ❖ ❖ ❖

Fifteen-year-old Ronald Johnson liked his life. His father, Ethan, was the foreman of Della-Starr Orchards, in Yakima Valley, Washington. After school and on weekends, he worked alongside his dad, under whose guidance Della-Starr had increased its harvest of apples by more than twenty percent. Ron, whose mother had died, lived with his father in a five-room house around a bend from the main house.

The only bad part about living at the orchard was all the unpleasantness that went on between the Turner sisters, Della and Starr, who owned the place named after them. The women were twins, but they were as different as night and day. Della was sweet and pleasant; Starr was tough, cranky, and always griping —especially about Della.

Ron had often heard the two sisters arguing, and lately it had been about the orchard. Starr wanted to buy it from Della, claiming she would give her a fair price. But Della refused, not wanting to leave the beautiful surroundings and the only home she had ever known.

51

One day, Ron overheard an especially hateful fight about just that, and over dinner that night, he told his dad.

"It's no secret that Starr wants sole ownership of the orchard," his father explained, "and so does Della. But this does not concern us, son. I have a job to do, and my only concern is doing it well." Getting up from the table, he gave Ron a pat on the shoulder. "I have to be up by four tomorrow. Think I'll turn in early."

By nine o'clock Ron's father was sound asleep. The dishes and housework done, Ron sat down with his schoolbooks at the kitchen table and tackled his math homework. The night was unusually warm and breezy. A soft wind played with the curtains framing the kitchen window, carrying with it the sound of voices from the main house . . . the forever arguing voices of Della and Starr.

Suddenly there was a scream, immediately followed by the thump of something falling. Ron ran to the open window, but from his angle he could see only the back porch of the main house. He listened carefully, then heard footsteps in the gravel drive. Then a moment of silence was shattered by the sound of glass breaking, followed by more footsteps in the gravel drive. Ron strained to hear, but only silence greeted his ears.

"Dad!" he yelled, running into his father's room. "Dad, something happened down at the main house!"

"What?" his father asked groggily, sitting up in bed.

Another scream sliced through the night. Then came Starr Turner's voice. "Stop! Help! Somebody stop him!"

"Call the sheriff, Dad!" yelled Ron, already out of the room. Running around the bend to the main house, he arrived just as Starr rushed out the front door to her pickup truck.

"Did you see him?" she demanded.

"Who?" asked Ron.

"The thief!" she practically screeched. "I'm going after him!"

The wheels of the pickup spun in the gravel, then the truck shot forward and roared off, bucking and jolting down the rutted dirt entry road to Della-Starr Orchards.

His heart racing, Ron made his way into the house. He found Della Turner, her blank eyes staring at nothing, lying on the living room carpet beneath a shattered window, her body sprinkled with broken glass. On the floor beside her was a heavy brass candlestick. Ron felt for a pulse. There was none. Della Turner was dead.

Starr had returned to the house and Ron's father had come over by the time Deputy Sheriff Gina Conway arrived on the scene.

"What happened here?" the deputy asked after briefly examining the body of Della Turner.

"It was a little after nine," said Starr. "My sister and I were in the den watching TV when we heard the sound of breaking glass. We both hurried into the living room. Standing there was a skinny man wearing a T-shirt, jeans, work gloves, and work boots."

"Would you recognize him if you saw him again?" asked Deputy Conway.

Starr nodded. "Yeah, especially his eyes. He had these weird, dark—almost black—eyes. When he saw us, he seemed to be as scared as we were. I think he thought no one was home. Anyway, Della screamed, and he grabbed that heavy brass candlestick and hit her with it. Then he took off, and I went after him."

"Officer Conway," said Ron, a bit nervously, "she's lying."

"How dare you!" bellowed Starr.

Deputy Conway turned to Ron. "What makes you think she's lying, young man?"

"Because what happened," explained Ron, "is Ms. Turner and her sister had an argument. I don't know if she planned it, or if it just happened in anger, but Starr Turner killed Della. Then she tried to make it look like a robbery. She even drove off in her pick-up in pursuit of a robber—a robber who didn't exist."

"But you weren't there," Ron's father broke in. "How could you know all this?"

"I heard it, Dad." Ron looked around the room. "And now, as I stand here, I can see it, too."

"See what?" sneered Starr.

"It's very hot tonight," Ron began, "and that's why some of the windows in this house are open. But that one—" he pointed at the broken window. "That one was closed. Why would a robber break a window to get in, when all he had to do was pull off the screen of an open one?"

"Because," said Starr, "he probably didn't notice

that the other windows were open. Anyway, he thought no one was home, so he didn't care if he made noise by breaking a window."

"How could anyone not think you were home, Ms. Turner? At nine o'clock, when the so-called robbery occurred, I could hear you loud and clear from my window, arguing with your sister."

"What you probably heard, you nosy brat," Starr scoffed, "was my sister and I yelling at the robber."

Ron remained totally calm. He had more evidence. "The important thing, Ms. Turner, is that you said the robber broke the glass, entered, and then killed your sister Della, right?"

"Yeah, that's right," Starr said defensively. "So?"

Ron smiled. "Well, what actually happened was the other way around. First you argued, then you hit your sister and killed her. After that, you went outside and smashed a window, to make it look like someone had broken in."

"And how are you going to prove such nonsense?" Starr insisted.

Ron turned to Deputy Conway. "Officer," he said, "please look at the body of Della Turner. There is glass on top the body. How could glass fall on top of the victim before she had fallen from the blow?"

Before Starr Turner fully realized what had happened, she was handcuffed, arrested on suspicion of murder, and read her rights.

"This doesn't prove anything!" Starr yelled, struggling against the cuffs, her once tough, impassive face now a mixture of fear, surprise, and puzzlement.

"What it proves," said Deputy Conway, smiling at

Ron, "is that this 'nosy brat,' as you referred to him, has just done a very nice job of keeping you from getting away with murder."

AN UNLUCKY NUMBER

❖ ❖ ❖ ❖ ❖ ❖ ❖

Brad and Marcy Dunlap and their mother had just arrived for a vacation in Orlando, Florida. So far, they were pretty miserable. It was the first week of August, right in the middle of summer, and the whole city was like a steam bath. By the time they arrived at their hotel, the Miramar Regency, sweat had made their clothes look as if they'd just been for a walk in the rain. A soothing blast of cool air greeted them as they followed the bellboy into the lobby.

"Pheew, what a relief!" Carrie Dunlap exclaimed as she and her children made their way to the registration desk.

"Thank goodness for air-conditioning," said twelve-year-old Brad.

"I wish they'd air-condition this whole state!" added Marcy, who was three years older.

Just then a dark-haired, good-looking man in a white suit made his way to the desk, and butted his way in front of them. The man, who had a thick mustache, seemed worried, and in a rush, and he got the immediate attention of the manager.

In his hand the man carried a beautiful cane with an ornately carved ivory hand-piece in the shape of a large spider. After a brief, whispered exchange of words, the man hurried off, and disappeared around a corner of the lobby.

"Pardon the interruption, Ms. Dunlap," said the manager, returning his attention to Brad and Marcy's mother. "Now, as I was saying, our elevators are out of order today. Only the service elevator is working, but I believe that will be sufficient for the needs of our guests. I assure you, the elevators will be working tomorrow."

While their mother was talking to the manager, Brad and Marcy wandered over to where a man was working on an open elevator, studying a tuft of multicolored wires.

"What's wrong with the elevators?" Brad asked the man.

"Afraid it's a bit too technical to explain to a little kid," the man sneered, not even looking up.

"Yeah," said Marcy, giving her brother a wink. "It probably is too technical for a kid to understand. Kids hardly know anything. But thank goodness we have grown-ups like you around who know everything."

"One of the many things I don't understand," said Brad, "is why the numbers of a lot of elevators skip the number thirteen."

The man gave Brad a you're-so-stupid look. "Kid, many hotels don't have a thirteenth floor. Thirteen's supposed to be unlucky."

"Oh, how interesting!" said Brad sarcastically. "I didn't know that about hotels, or even that thirteen is unlucky. You wouldn't happen to know why thirteen is considered—"

"Look, kid," groaned the man. "I got work to do."

"Of course," said Marcy. "We won't take up more of your time. Thank you for illuminating our childish minds."

They burst out laughing, then walked back to their mother, who had just finished registering. "We're all set, kids," she said. And with that, they all followed the bellboy, pulling a cart stacked high with their suitcases, to the service elevator at the back of the hotel.

As the heavy metal doors rolled open, Brad's eyes grew wide. "Wow, this is a totally humongous—and weird—elevator," said Brad, looking all around what was almost the size of a small room.

The doors rolled closed, and the bellboy pushed the button for the fourteenth floor.

"What's that button up there for?" Brad asked the bellboy, as the elevator started it's ascent.

"Never noticed it before," the young man answered with a shrug, looking at the small button in the ceiling Brad was pointing to.

"Kind of an odd place to put a button, isn't it?" Marcy remarked. "It's so high nobody can reach it."

The elevator stopped and Marcy and Brad followed the bellboy, who unlocked the door to their room and showed them around. As soon as he left, Brad and Marcy plopped on the bed and, using the TV remote control, began flipping through the channels.

"Hey," Marcy said, pointing to a familiar face as it flashed past on the screen. "That's the man in the white suit who was in the lobby!" She quickly backed up to the station.

"For years, drug lord Elio Araña has eluded police," the anchorwoman on the national news show was saying. "He has been spotted in Orlando many times, but somehow he always manages to disappear."

"Are you sure that's the man you saw?" asked Brad.

"Yeah, and I'm sure about his name, too" said Marcy. "The guy the cops are after is named Araña. In Spanish, araña means 'spider.' Remember the walking stick the man at the registration desk was carrying?" she asked excitedly. "It had the design of a spider on the handle."

"So, this big-shot drug dealer's right in our hotel!" said Brad, jumping on the bed. "He's—"

"I'm going to go take a shower, kids," their mother called from the bathroom. "Are you just going to watch TV?"

Brad and Marcy nodded vigorously. They knew instinctively not to tell their mom anything, or she'd make them stay out of it. That's why they waited for the shower to go on before they dialed the police.

Five minutes later they met Detectives Edith Barrister and Ronald Savelini down in the lobby. The detectives questioned the manager, who said he'd never seen Araña.

Marcy pulled Detective Barrister aside. "The manager is lying," she said. "That means he must be one of the people who helps Araña keep escaping."

Barrister and Savelini went from floor to floor on the elevators, which were now back in service. Finding nothing, they decided to set up a stakeout in the lobby.

After three days of staking out the Miramar Regency, there had been no trace of Elio Araña. Barrister and Savelini were ready to give up, and Brad and Marcy were beside themselves. With only one night left before leaving Orlando, they decided to confide in their mother.

"We know this guy is somewhere in the hotel," Marcy said to her mother, as the three of them packed for a morning flight the next day. "He probably knows he's being staked out."

"Yeah, and the manager here is working with him," added Brad. "Somehow he's tipping Araña off. He'll never come out until the coast is clear."

"So the question is," said their mother, suddenly interested, "where in this hotel would be the best place to hide?"

"Let's think back to the one time we saw Araña," suggested Mary. "He hurried in—carrying that walking stick—and talked to the manager. Then he headed around the corner to the service elevator."

"Which," Brad pointed out, "has that weird button on the ceiling, and—" He jumped up from the bed. "Mom," he said, trying to stay calm, "Marcy and I will be right back." Then, before his mother could protest, he dragged his sister out the door.

On the way down to the lobby, Brad explained to Marcy what he'd figured out. There, talking a mile a minute to Detectives Barrister and Savelini, he convinced them to examine the service elevator.

Marcy pushed the button, and the four waited for the oversize elevator. When it came, Brad suggested that the detectives press the tiny button on the ceiling.

"It can't be reached," said Savelini.

"Exactly," said Brad. "Why don't you give me a boost?"

Savelini did as he was asked, and after Brad pressed the button, the elevator started going up.

Passing the number twelve, the elevator suddenly jerked to a stop—and its rear door rolled open, onto a sumptuous penthouse that took up the entire floor. Elio Araña, the hotel manager, and the elevator repairman stared wide-eyed at their unexpected guests . . . and at the guns in the hands of the detectives.

"Welcome to the thirteenth floor," announced

Marcy, "which Mr. Spider here reaches by pushing a button with his cane. Meanwhile, Mr. Repairman has rigged all the regular elevators to pass right by this floor." She paused, and waved her hand in a grand gesture toward the last man in the room. "And finally, we have Mr. Hotel Manager, who probably set up this clever little hiding place."

Brad walked up to the elevator repairman. "Sir," he said, "you sure were right."

"About what?" muttered the man angrily.

"About a thirteenth floor. A hotel shouldn't have one. You see, they really are unlucky, very unlucky."

65

THE SUNKEN
BOAT

❖ ❖ ❖ ❖ ❖ ❖ ❖

Thirteen-year-old Gary Isley sat mesmerized in his third-period class as he listened to Mr. O'Toole, his history teacher, talk about the sinking of the Titanic.

"This is an actual cap worn by a British officer on the night the Titanic hit an iceberg," said Mr. O'Toole, holding up a dark blue visored cap. He then passed around several photographs of the launching of the ship, along with his coin collection. "Most of the coins you see there," he explained, "were minted around 1912, the year the ship sank."

When everyone had had a chance to see all the items, Mr. O'Toole turned out the lights and the class watched the second half of the movie about the famous ship. Instantly, the screen filled with a scene of passengers battling to get into lifeboats, and Gary was fascinated. He had never seen the movie before, but he had read a book by the same title, A Night to Remember, and had been anxious to see the film version. He glanced at his teacher in the darkened room. Barely visible, Mr. O'Toole placed the cap, the coin collection, and photos on a back table, then took a

67

seat at his desk.

Later, during the movie, Gary noticed a student slip out the back door of the class. He couldn't see who it was, only that it was a girl. Why didn't she ask for a pass? Gary wondered. And why didn't Mr. O'Toole notice her sneaking out?

Not until the movie was over and the lights were flipped on did Gary understand why Mr. O'Toole hadn't seen anything. He had dozed off during the movie. The lights going on—and a few snickers—startled him awake.

"Sorry, guys," the embarrassed teacher said, quickly rising to his feet and stopping the projector. "That's the third time I've seen this movie today, and I—" He stopped himself midsentence. His eyes were

on the back table. "My coin collection is missing!" he said, obviously upset. "No one leaves this room until I have an explanation."

Gary raised his hand. "Someone already has left the room, Mr. O'Toole, but it was really dark, and I couldn't see who it was."

"I saw Judy Kowitz slip something into her gym bag during the movie," said Irene Morris.

Everyone knew Irene and Judy didn't like each other. Among other things, they both liked Bill Walters, and it was Judy he took to the spring dance.

"And after she put something in her bag," continued Irene, "I saw her sneak out with it."

"I did not!" said Judy angrily, jumping to her feet. "I never left the room! I've never stolen any—" She suddenly stopped and looked frantically under her desk. "Hey! My gym bag is gone!"

"Gee, what a coincidence," sneered Irene. "And what a coincidence that you're a coin collector, too."

"I didn't take it!" cried Judy. Fighting back tears, she ran from the room.

By first period the next day, just about everyone in the school knew that the coin collection had been found in Judy Kowitz's locker in her gym bag. Judy pleaded her innocence to her classmates, to Mr. O'Toole, and to the principal. She said that she and Irene had once been friends, and had even shared the same locker, until a few weeks ago. "That's when Bill took me to the dance and not her," Judy explained. "Irene got really upset. I even caught her stealing money from my purse."

The two incidents quickly ended the friendship, and Irene had gotten into a lot of trouble when Judy's mother called Irene's mother and told her about the theft.

"Obviously," Judy told everyone who would listen, "Irene took the coins and planted them in my gym bag to get even."

Irene, of course, denied the accusation. "Well, I think it's disgusting that a former friend would steal something," she said, "and then try to blame it on me."

When third-period history came around, the atmosphere in Mr. O'Toole's classroom was strained and tense. Mr. O'Toole said nothing about the coin collection, but simply began his lesson for the day.

Gary raised his hand. "Mr. O'Toole," he said, "I don't know whether Judy or Irene—or somebody else—took the coins. But I'm sure I can find out who did."

"And how are you going to do that, Gary?" asked Mr. O'Toole, clearly skeptical.

Gary went to the front of the class. "I want everyone to write his or her name on a piece of paper," he said, as he turned to the chalkboard. "Then write the answer to this question."

The class was silent as Gary wrote: WHY DID THE TITANIC'S MUSICIANS ALL SQUEEZE INTO ONE LIFEBOAT?

After three or four minutes, Gary collected the answers. He read Irene's first: "Because they were friends and were looking out for each other by being together." Then he read Judy's answer. "They never got in a lifeboat. They played music to comfort the people on the sinking ship, and they went down with the Titanic." At random, Gary read other answers. But he really didn't have to read any more to solve the mystery of who took Mr. O'Toole's coins.

Gary put down the answers, grinned at his classmates, and launched into his explanation. "Judy's locker—the combination of which both she and Irene know, since they once shared it—is a long walk from this classroom. In fact, it's almost all the way across campus. Still, there was plenty of time during the movie to slip out of class with the coins and hide them. There was also enough time to miss the part of the movie about the musicians. So," Gary concluded, "the person who stole the coins is the one who got the answer wrong."

Instantly, all eyes were on Irene, who looked like she wanted to crawl in a hole and hide.

Mr. O'Toole smiled at Gary. Then he turned his attention to Irene. "Sorry, young lady, but it looks to me like somebody just sank your boat."

THE RADAR-BRAIN DETECTIVE

❖ ❖ ❖ ❖ ❖ ❖ ❖

Stacy Chang loved her summer job at the Pike City police station, in Oregon. Sheriff Gladstone was a sweet old man, but he was also extremely messy and old-fashioned. Stacy's job was to keep things in order, to answer phone calls, and to operate the computer.

Lately there had been a mysterious rash of kidnappings. The first to be abducted was an eight-year-old boy named Ronnie Devon. Neither Sheriff Gladstone nor his two deputies had a single clue as to the boy's whereabouts, and for seven days he had remained missing. Finally, the sheriff turned to his last hope—a psychic named Edward Singer.

A small, slender man with close-cropped hair, Singer claimed, somewhat self-consciously, that in his native Britain, he had been known as the "Radar-Brain Detective." He also claimed he had solved over a hundred kidnapping cases.

Singer had held some of Ronnie's toys and clothing.

Then, eyes closed and as though in a trance, he had mumbled that the boy had been taken by a burly man with black hair. Ronnie, he had said, was alive and being kept in the cellar of a two-story brown house with many rose bushes in front. Then, upon opening his eyes, Singer had insisted that he should accept no fee—which was three thousand dollars—unless the boy was found alive and unharmed.

The next day, the brown house with the rose bushes was located, and Ronnie was reunited with his sobbing parents. Once again, Singer was lauded as a genius, and he graciously accepted his three-thousand dollar fee.

In the next few weeks, there were four more kidnappings. All of the cases were much the same. Never was the child hurt in any way; always the kidnapper was described as a big, dark-haired man; always he made a ransom demand of a hundred thousand dollars. Not once was the kidnapper successful in collecting the money, and never was he spotted by the police, let alone captured.

In addition to all of this, each abducted child described the kidnapper as having an accomplice—an unattractive woman with long blond hair who always wore green-framed dark glasses and lots of makeup. The woman, each child pointed out, never said a word.

Edward Singer continued to help find the children, but he always refused to go with the police on the search. "It might help the investigation if you came along," Sheriff Gladstone would often implore the odd psychic, but Singer said it made him too nervous to go to the crime scene.

"What if the child is dead?" he would explain. "That would be too much for me."

Instead, after turning on his "psychic sight," as he referred to it, and getting a mental picture of the location, Singer would wait in the police station while the sheriff and his deputies searched the town.

For a time, there were no more abductions, and Sheriff Gladstone concluded the kidnappers had moved to another area. He was angry that he hadn't caught them, but he was relieved that at least the kids in his town were safe.

But then it happened again. A nine-year-old girl, Nina Pandelli, taking a shortcut home from school, had disappeared.

Once again, Edward Singer was called in.

Stacy was fascinated as the slender, dark-haired man sat on a hard-backed chair in Sheriff Gladstone's office. Eyes closed, with his long, delicate, almost feminine-looking fingers, he ran his hands over the little girl's teddy bear and her favorite jacket. But this time he had no luck.

"Nothing's coming through," he said sadly, as he picked a strand of blond hair from his turtleneck sweater. "It's so frustrating. I think of my own little girl and what it would do to me to lose her." Getting up dejectedly and heading for the door, he promised to return in the morning.

Intrigued by Singer, Stacy Chang ran his name through the computer. She found that Singer, as he had claimed, had been born and raised in Britain. He was dubbed the "Radar-Brain Detective" because he had indeed solved a number of cases, most of them involving missing children. Stacy was a bit surprised, however, to learn that the man had once been arrested for burglary—but had been acquitted. She also noted that Singer was listed as unmarried with no dependents.

Maybe he had a child who died, thought Stacy, remembering how Singer had mentioned his own little girl. Or maybe he's fond of a friend's daughter who he has come to refer to as his own. Or maybe he's just a nut case.

The next day, Sheriff Gladstone gave Singer an old tennis shoe that had belonged to the missing child. Singer went into a trance, began rocking back and forth, and finally spoke.

"I see an apartment, blue with white trim," he

mumbled. "And there's a brick walkway. Yes," he said firmly. "The little girl has definitely walked on those bricks."

The Sheriff and his two deputies were off in a flash, looking for the place. For a short while Singer just sat, idly fiddling with a pair of sunglasses, looking exhausted as he always did after one of his "psychic breakthroughs." Then, as he usually did after recovering from the trauma of it all, he made a phone call. The message was always brief, and he said pretty much the same thing: "I really think I've located the child. The police are looking now. I'll wait until the sheriff gets back to see how it went."

Just after noon, Sheriff Gladstone and one deputy returned—with the young girl. The kidnappers had escaped, and once again, although a ransom had been left in the designated place, it had not been picked up.

"Don't give him anything!" Stacy nearly shouted when she saw Sheriff Gladstone start to write Singer a check. "He's one of the kidnappers!"

The sheriff stared open-mouthed.

"I beg your pardon, young lady," Singer said, folding his arms across his chest.

"This better be good, Stacy," the sheriff said. "Mr. Singer has been quite a help to us."

"My first clue," said Stacy, "was the long blond hairs that are often on Singer's clothes. I believe they come from the wig he wears as part of a disguise. He's the unattractive blonde who works with the burly man, and she never speaks because she's a man!"

"This is preposterous!" shouted Singer.

"And remember the green-framed sunglasses this

supposed female accomplice wears?" Stacy asked, not skipping a beat. "Look what Mr. Singer is holding right now."

All eyes went to the glasses in Singer's hands.

Stacy took a deep breath. "Finally," she said, turning to the sheriff, "you never catch the big, burly man because Singer tips him off—right after you leave the station."

"I'm a true psychic," protested Singer. "This is nonsense. I have a gift. I would never—"

"No!" insisted Stacy. "It's exactly as I said, and I can prove it."

"Go on, Stacy," said Sheriff Gladstone. "I'd like to hear what you have to say."

"I assume," Stacy said, "that your other deputy is still at the apartment where the missing girl was found."

"Yes," said the sheriff. "Deputy O'Reilly is there, dusting for prints."

"The last call made from this office," said Stacy, "was made by Singer." Stacy picked up the phone, punched the redial button, and held up the receiver for all to hear. After two rings, a familiar voice came through loud and clear: "O'Reilly speaking. May I help you?"

"But what's that prove?" Singer said, beginning to sound a little flustered.

"What it proves," said Sheriff Gladstone, "is that you called right from this office to the apartment where the child was being held. Stacy must be right. You were warning your partner that we were on the way." He paused and scratched his head. "Ransom money wasn't your game. It was too big of a risk, since it's in picking up the ransom that kidnappers are most likely to get caught. What you were after was the three-thousand dollar 'psychic' fee."

Stacy looked at the sweating, nervous Edward Singer. "Now, Mr. Radar-Brain Detective, maybe the sheriff will go easier on you if you turn on your 'radar' one last time and tell us where your accomplice is. I doubt you'll need to go into a trance for that."

FRAMED

❖ ❖ ❖ ❖ ❖ ❖ ❖

Andrea Meadows was nervous as she and her mother drove along River Front Drive. It would be her first day of work at the Milwaukee Gallery of Fine Arts. Her mother, a security guard at the gallery, had gotten her a part-time job as a file clerk during summer vacation.

"A few butterflies?" her mother said, stifling a yawn.

"I'll be okay," said Andrea, smiling.

Her mother returned the smile and rubbed her red eyes. Andrea could see how tired she was. Her mother had worked from 10:00 A.M. to 7:00 P.M. yesterday and now would do another full shift to get overtime pay. It was hard for a single parent to make ends meet, especially on a security guard's salary.

"I wonder what's going on," her mother said as they pulled into the parking lot behind the gallery and saw that most of the snow-draped cars were police cars. Her mother quickly parked, and they hurried inside, into the staff lounge.

"What's with the police brigade?" her mother asked Nick Crowley, the caretaker, who looked like he was about a hundred years old.

"There's been a robbery," said Nick. "Someone made off with the Magritte last night."

"The Magritte!" exclaimed Andrea's mother. "Oh no!"

René Magritte's The Healer, Andrea knew, was the prize of the gallery's collection—and worth upward of six million. Her mind raced as she followed her mother and Nick into the security office of the gallery, dominated by dozens of monitor panels, each fixed on a different room or part of the building. One of the rooms showed where the Magritte had been on display. In its place was an empty frame.

"How could this happen?" cried Beatrice Delacourte, the owner of the gallery, dabbing her eyes as she clattered into the room on spike high heels.

A rugged-looking man in a sports jacket followed Beatrice. He immediately stepped around her and walked up to Andrea's mother. "Are you Julia Meadows?" he asked, flashing a badge.

Andrea watched her mother nod and quietly answer yes.

"I'm Lieutenant Stone," the man said, pulling a chair out. "Would you like to sit down? I need to ask you a few questions." He took out a pad and pencil, then sat down across from Andrea's mother. "Yesterday you were the only security guard on duty between 10:00 A.M. and 7:00 P.M. Is that correct?"

"Yes," said Julia Meadows in a flat tone. "That was my shift."

"And after closing time, 4:00 P.M., was anyone else in the gallery?" the lieutenant asked.

Andrea listened carefully as her mother explained

that Nick Crowley and Ms. Delacourte had been in the gallery until closing. "After that," her mother stated with certainty in her voice, "the cleaning crew was here from 4:00 to 6:00 P.M.—no one else."

Stone scratched his head and tapped his pencil on the table. "We have a rather puzzling situation," he said after a moment. "The Magritte painting was in a locked room—a room that was locked after the painting vanished. Do you have any explanation?"

"None," said Julia Meadows. "It was in the room the last time I made my rounds. That was right after the cleaning crew left . . . about five-thirty."

Beatrice Delacourte shook her head sadly and looked coldly at Andrea's mother. "I'm trying not to think the worst, Julia," she said. Then turning to Lieutenant Stone, she added, "I've already contacted the papers and posted twenty-five thousand dollars for the painting's return. As you can see, I'm willing to do just about anything to have my Magritte back."

Stone nodded and looked sternly at Julia Meadows. "I have something I'd like you all to watch," he said, reaching across the table and turning on a monitor connected to a VCR. "This surveillance video was taken of you, Ms. Meadows, leaving work last night at 7:14 P.M. In it, as you can see, you are carrying a long, rectangular box. Such a box could be used to carry a rolled-up painting, could it not?"

"Yes," agreed Julia Meadows. "But the fact is, it contained flowers."

The lieutenant raised an eyebrow. "Flowers?"

"I didn't understand how I came to be carrying flowers home either," Andrea's mother explained. "But a little after five-thirty yesterday afternoon, a delivery boy arrived with a dozen long-stemmed roses. There was no card, but my name and the museum's address were written on the box. And that is what I was taking home, Lieutenant Stone—a box of flowers."

Stone made a few notations in his pad, then changed the cassette in the VCR. "I'd like you to watch something else," he said, pushing the play button. "This video shows the room at 5:29 P.M.," he said. "As you can see, the Magritte was in its frame. Please watch what happens."

Andrea carefully studied the monitor along with everyone else. The time, displayed in the lower left-hand corner of the video, ticked off slowly as she saw a door opening, and then, for an instant, her mother's profile. Seconds later, the painting was gone. The time on the monitor had flipped from 5:29 to 5:48 P.M.

"Obviously," said Stone, stopping the VCR, "several minutes of the tape have been erased. Isn't the security guard on duty in charge of the tapes, Ms. Meadows?"

All eyes turned to Andrea's mother.

"And to think I trusted you so completely," wailed Beatrice Delacourte.

"Hard to believe," said Nick, shaking his head.

"Excuse me, Officer Stone," Andrea said quietly. "But could I see the tape again?"

Stone shrugged. "I don't see why not, young lady. But I'm afraid your mother has some evidence against her." He rewound the tape and replayed it. Once again, Andrea watched with the others as the Magritte appeared on the screen one minute and was gone the next.

But this time when the tape ended, Andrea sat back and smiled. "I think I know how the painting was taken," she said confidently. "And I also know where it is. Please, Officer Stone, play the tape just once more—but this time, in slow motion."

Puzzled, Stone rewound the tape and pressed the button for slow motion.

"Watch the carpeting," said Andrea, as the scene reappeared in front of everyone. "There are no footprints in it when my mom opens the door—probably because the cleaning crew had just vacuumed it." She paused. "Now comes the big gap in the tape. And after that there are two sets of prints." Andrea turned to her mother. "Mom, what shoes did you wear yesterday?" she asked.

"The same as today." Julia Meadows extended her foot. She was wearing walking shoes with a waffle print on the soles. "I wear them every day, because they're so comfortable."

Andrea turned to Lieutenant Stone. "Could we just look at the carpeting one more time?" she asked.

Stone nodded and rewound the tape.

"See how my mother's footprints go straight through the room?" Andrea asked everyone. "But notice that there's a second set of prints that lead straight to the Magritte . . . then to the painting to the right of it. Now, notice how that painting is slightly tilted." Andrea grinned proudly. "My guess is that the Magritte is behind the tilted painting, and that the thief planned to return for it later."

Stone hurried from the room. Several minutes

later he returned with the Magritte in hand. "I'm very impressed, young lady!" he exclaimed. "It was right where you said it would be."

"But who took the painting—and hid it?" asked Nick.

This time Andrea took it upon herself to operate the VCR. She stepped forward and rewound the tape, then punched "stop-hold," followed by "zoom." Frozen, close-up, were the prints in the carpet. "See the second set of prints?" she asked. "They were made by someone wearing high heels . . . just like the ones you're wearing, Ms. Delacourte."

"This is outrageous," stammered Beatrice Delacourte, as everyone looked at her feet. "Why would I steal my own painting?"

"Simple," said Andrea. "You collect the insurance money and resell the Magritte on the black market."

"And how about the flowers—that long box?" asked Nick. "That was just a setup, wasn't it?"

"I believe it was, Mr. Crowley," said Stone. "And I'd bet my badge that if we called the florist who delivered those flowers, we'd find that they were sent by one Beatrice Delacourte."

After Lieutenant Stone read Beatrice Delacourte her rights, he took her arm and began to lead her out of the room. "Julia, I—" she began, turning toward Andrea's mother.

But before Ms. Delacourte finished her sentence, Andrea stepped forward and glared into the woman's eyes. "You owe my mother an apology, and me twenty-five thousand dollars."

"What do you mean—twenty-five thousand

dollars?!" Beatrice Delacourte blurted out, then chuckled. "But whatever for?"

Andrea grinned from ear to ear. "That's the reward you posted for finding your painting," she said. "A painting you stole yourself and *I* recovered!"

THE MAN IN THE GLASS BUBBLE

❖ ❖ ❖ ❖ ❖ ❖ ❖

Jason Montrose?" said the little man in the dark suit at the front door of the apartment.

Thirteen-year-old Jason Montrose nodded. "Yes, that's me."

"Jason, I am from the First National Bank of Menlo Park," said the man, drawing a large, brown, old-looking envelope from his briefcase. "This is for you. We've been holding it in our vault for sixty-three years."

"But I'm only thirteen," said Jason. "How could something be held for me longer than I've been alive?"

The man handed the envelope to Jason. "I'm afraid I don't know. I'm only following instructions. Good day to you, young man," he said, and hurried off.

"Hey, wait a second," called Jason. "What's this all about?"

But the man was already headed down the apartment-house stairs.

Just then, Peggy, Jason's eleven-year-old sister,

walked in from the kitchen, munching on corn chips. "Who was that?" she asked.

"I don't know," said Jason as he shut the door. "He gave me this envelope and said it's been held in a vault for me . . . for sixty-three years!"

"How weird," Peggy said, furrowing her brow in thought. "Let me see it."

Jason pulled the envelope away from her grasp. "Wait a minute. I haven't even seen it," he said, studying the odd handwriting on the outside. "To the eldest descendant of John Kruesi," he read out loud. "To be delivered on my death day, October 18, three score and three after the year of our Lord 1931."

"Who's John Kruesi?" asked Peggy.

"I don't know any John Kruesi," replied Jason. "But Kruesi was Grandma's last name before she got married."

He broke the seal on the envelope, and out dropped two keys. One was small and had a tag with the number 211 printed on it. The other key was large and old-fashioned looking. There was also a yellowing letter in the envelope. Again, Jason read out loud: "I've been dead sixty-three years. That's long enough, don't you think? Come and find me. We'll both be surprised." The letter was signed "The Wizard."

"Total weirdness!" exclaimed Peggy.

"Yeah, and written by a total weirdo," said Jason.

Peggy took the keys from him. "What do you suppose these open?"

"The man who delivered the envelope said he was from the First National Bank of Menlo Park," said Jason, "so I guess the keys open something there." He went over to the bookcase and pulled out an atlas. He flipped to the index and ran his finger down a list of names. "There are two places called Menlo Park in the United States. One is here in New Jersey. The other is out in California."

"So which one was he talking about?"

"Probably the one here in New Jersey, since the man had an eastern accent," Jason said, turning to a map of New Jersey. "Hey, Menlo Park's only about twenty miles from here!"

With Peggy on his heels, Jason ran upstairs to their father's office. "Dad's always taking trains on business and probably has a schedule around here somewhere," he said, rummaging through some papers on the desk.

"There," said Peggy, pointing to a train schedule tacked up on a bulletin board. She glanced down the list of trains. "The next one leaves in an hour."

"Perfect!" Jason exclaimed. "We can ride our bikes to the station in thirty minutes. Are you with me?"

Peggy nodded eagerly, and they were off.

"So here we are in beautiful Menlo Park, looking for a dead guy who writes letters," said Jason as he and Peggy got off the train.

Peggy giggled nervously. "So where does he hang out—at the cemetery?"

"Could be," Jason said, looking at the small key with the tag attached to it. "But I'll bet we'll learn more at the post office. The numbers on this tag probably belong to a mailbox."

91

After a few inquiries, Jason and Peggy learned that the main post office was just a few blocks away. They raced over and were soon standing before box 211. Holding his breath, Jason slipped in the key.

"It fits!" he said, turning the key and opening the box.

Inside was another letter. Jason read it out loud to Peggy: "Tell the doors at 371 Rome Street that Mary had a little lamb."

Jason and Peggy looked at each other and shrugged. "What does a nursery rhyme have to do with all this?" Peggy asked.

"Only one way to find out," said Jason.

Getting directions from a passerby, they made their way down Rome Street. The house at 371 was old and run-down, and its windows were boarded up.

Peggy shuddered. "I don't know, Jason. This place looks kind of creepy."

"Look, we've come this far," Jason said, inserting the other key that had been in the envelope into the lock of the heavy wood door.

There was a click, and the door opened to reveal a pair of huge steel doors.

"Now what?" asked Peggy.

Jason faced the doors. "Mary had a little lamb," he said loudly.

Instantly, the twin doors slid open like an elevator. Looking at each other in wonder, Jason and Peggy stepped in, and the doors rolled shut behind them.

Within seconds, they were surrounded by a loud hum, and they began to descend. Then suddenly they stopped, and the doors opened onto a large room. In

the center of the room was a brightly lit glass bubble about the size of an elephant.

"Wow!" Jason and Peggy gasped in unison.

Inside the glass bubble was an old man dressed in old-fashioned clothes. He looked as though he were alive, but his eyes were closed and he was neither moving nor breathing.

Stepping closer, Jason and Peggy could hear a droning hum. They could also see that the glass dome was connected to an engine. On the engine were the words PUSH TO END CYCLE.

His hands trembling, Jason pushed the button.

Suddenly, the man started breathing. His eyes moved and turned toward Jason and Peggy. He smiled, then pushed a control with his finger. A glass door slid open, and he stepped out.

"What year is it?" asked the old man.

Stammering, Peggy told him.

"Oh, how wonderful!" he cried happily. "It worked!" Then seeing the confusion in both Peggy's and Jason's eyes, he smiled. "Please," he said, "allow me to explain. You see, in 1931 I invented my life-storage machine. Being an old man anyway, I decided to test it on myself. I built it, got in, and John turned it on. Not until you pushed the button and ended the cycle have I been aware of anything that has been going on for the past sixty-three years."

"John? Do you mean John Kruesi?"

"Yes, John was my shop foreman. And he also helped me set up my little experiment. You see, in 1931 I was supposed to have died. A fake funeral was held, one in which they played 'Mary Had a Little Lamb,' the first words spoken on my favorite invention."

Suddenly, Jason knew who the man was. It was a man whose picture he had seen many times in history books—a man who had been one of the greatest inventors of all time—a man who was known as the Wizard of Menlo Park. Jason gasped. The man was . . .

"Allow me to introduce myself," said the man, stepping forward and taking Jason's hand. "Edison's the name. Thomas Edison. And you?"